NOTE TO PARENTS

Learning to read is an important skill for all children. It is a big milestone that you can help your child reach. The Richard Scarry Easy Reader program is designed to support you and your child through this process. Developed by reading specialists, each book in the series includes carefully selected words and sentence structures to help children advance from beginner to intermediate to proficient readers.

Here are some tips to keep in mind as you read these books with your child:

First, preview the book together. Read the title. Then look at the cover. Ask your child, "What is happening on the cover? What do you think this book is about?"

Next, skim through the pages of the book and look at the illustrations. This will help your child use the illustrations to understand the story.

Then encourage your child to read. If he or she stumbles over words, try some of these strategies:

- **Use the pictures as clues**
- **Point out words that are repeated**
- **Sound out difficult words**
- **Break up bigger words into smaller chunks**
- **Use the context to lend meaning**

Finally, find out if your child understands what he or she is reading. After you have finished reading, ask, "What happened in this book?"

Above all, understand that each child learns to read at a different rate. Make sure to praise your young reader and provide encouragement along the way!

LEVEL 1

Introduce Your Child to Reading

Simple words and simple sentences encourage beginning readers to sound out words.

LEVEL 2

Your Child Starts to Read

Slightly more difficult words in simple sentences help new readers build confidence.

LEVEL 3

Your Child Reads with Help

More complex words and sentences and longer text lengths help young readers reach reading proficiency.

RICHARD SCARRY'S
Great Big Schoolhouse
Readers

Hop, Hop, and Away!

Illustrated by Huck Scarry
Written by Erica Farber

STERLING

New York / London
www.sterlingpublishing.com/kids

Today is show-and-tell.

Huckle packed his backpack.

Huckle packed his lunch.

Huckle packed his pet frog.

Hop, hop, and away!

Huckle's frog hopped away.

Lowly got the frog.

Phew!

Good job, Lowly!

Huckle went to school.

Hop, hop, and away!

Huckle's frog hopped away.

Skip got the frog.

Thank you, Skip!

It was time for show-and-tell.

Show & Tell

Arthur showed
his ant farm.

Ella showed her fancy doll.

Bridget had a whistle.

Bridget blew it.

10

Hop, hop, and away!

Huckle's frog hopped away.

It hopped on Ella. Oh, no!

Huckle got his frog.
It was not his turn.

Lowly was next.
He told a joke.

Molly showed a book.

Skip had a big ball.

He bounced the ball.

Bam! Bam!

Frances had a volcano.

She put stuff into it.

At last it was Huckle's turn.

He showed his frog.

BOOM! went the volcano.

BOOM! BOOM!

Lava went up in the air.

Lava went all over.

Bridget blew
her whistle.

Hop, hop, and away!

Huckle's frog hopped away.

It hopped on Skip.

Bam went Skip's ball.

The ball hit Molly's book.

The book hit the ant farm.

BOOM! CRASH!

Hop, hop, and away!
Huckle's frog hopped
on Miss Honey.

She smiled.

Show & Te

hen it was time to clean up.

his was the best show-and-tell ever!

STERLING and the distinctive Sterling logo are registered trademarks of Sterling Publishing Co., Inc.

Library of Congress Cataloging-in-Publication Data Available

Lot #: 10 9 8 7 6 5 4 3 2 1
03/11
Published by Sterling Publishing Co., Inc.
387 Park Avenue South, New York, NY 10016

In association with JB Publishing, Inc.
121 West 27th Street, Suite 902, New York, NY 10001

Distributed in Canada by Sterling Publishing
c/o Canadian Manda Group, 165 Dufferin Street
Toronto, Ontario, Canada M6K 3H6
Distributed in the United Kingdom by GMC Distribution Services
Castle Place, 166 High Street, Lewes, East Sussex, England BN7 1XU
Distributed in Australia by Capricorn Link (Australia) Pty. Ltd.
P.O. Box 704, Windsor, NSW 2756, Australia

produced by ●JR Sansevere

Sterling ISBN: 978-1-4027-8448-4 (hardcover)
               978-1-4027-7318-1 (paperback)

For information about custom editions, special sales, premium and corporate purchases, please contact Sterling Special Sales Department at 800-805-5489 or specialsales@sterlingpublishing.com.

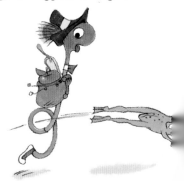

RICHARD SCARRY'S
Great Big Schoolhouse
Readers

One of the best-selling children's author/illustrators of all time, Richard Scarry has taught generations of children about the world around them—from the alphabet to counting, identifying colors, and even exploring a day at school.

Though Scarry's books are educational, they are beloved for their charming characters, wacky sense of humor, and frenetic energy. Scarry considered himself an entertainer first, and an educator second. He once said, "Everything has an educational value if you look for it. But it's the FUN I want to get across."

A prolific artist, Richard Scarry created more than 300 books, and they have sold over 200 million copies worldwide and have been translated into 30 languages. Richard Scarry died in 1994, but his incredible legacy continues with new books illustrated by his son, Huck Scarry.